by Rowan Obach
illustrated by Laurie Conley

SCHOOL PUBLISHERS

Printed in China

ISBN 10: 0-15-358408-4
ISBN 13: 978-0-15-358408-4

Ordering Options
ISBN 10: 0-15-358356-8 (Grade K On-Level Collection)
ISBN 13: 978-0-15-358356-8 (Grade K On-Level Collection)
ISBN 10: 0-15-360660-6 (package of 5)
ISBN 13: 978-0-15-360660-1 (package of 5)

4 5 6 7 8 9 10 0940 15 14 13 12 11 10 09

Look at the box.
The box will go up.

Look at the box.
It will come down.

Look in the box!

What will I do?
I can not win!

Do not look sad.
I can fix this.

I will mix it up.

See, I did fix it!